DOG DAY

Sarah Hayes

Pictures by
Hannah Broadway

Farrar Straus Giroux
New York

Printed and bound in Thailand by Imago

Produced by Brubaker & Ford Ltd.
London and New York

First edition, 2008

10 9 8 7 6 5 4 3 2 1

www.fsgkidsbooks.com

Library of Congress Control Number: 2007940454

ISBN-13: 978-0-374-31810-9
ISBN-10: 0-374-31810-7

For Hannah —S.H.

For Calypso, Dan, Francis, Iris,
Joseph & Mikey Macaroni.
Big thanks to D&B, Robbie,
Daniel & Mr. Pips —H.B.

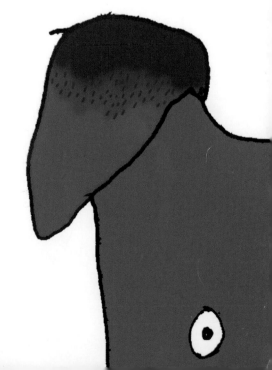

Here is Ben.

Here is Ben's
lunchbox.

Here is Ben's classroom.

Here is Ellie.

Ben's new teacher
is a dog!

Riff wags his tail.

Wag
Wag

Ben wags his bottom.

Wag
Wag

Wag
Wag

Wag

Wag
Wag

Wag
Wag

They all wag their bottoms.

Now Riff scratches his ear.

Scratch

Ellie scratches her ear.

Scratch

Ben scratches under his chin.

Scratch scratch

They all scratch all over.

Scratch

Scratch

Scratch

Scratch

Scratch scratch

Scratch

What's next?

shake

shake
shake

shake

shake

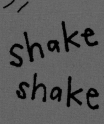

shake

shake
shake

Shaking.

Riff shakes all over.

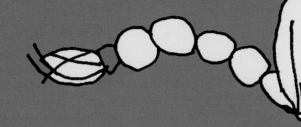

They all shake all over.

What's that smell?

It's Riff's lunch.

Riff has dog food
for lunch.

Ben and Ellie
have sandwiches.

Ellie throws a ball.

Ben runs and brings it back.

What's next?

Time for a nap.

Then Riff sniffs.

sniff
sniff

Ben and Ellie sniff.

Someone's coming.

Oh, no!

It's Mrs. Pink,
the principal.

Mrs. Pink wants to hear about their day.